SAVED BY

Grace

Saved By *Grace*

Joseph Kaczuska Jr

Xulon Press

Xulon Press
2301 Lucien Way #415
Maitland, FL 32751
407.339.4217
www.xulonpress.com

© 2023 by Joseph Kaczuska Jr

All rights reserved solely by the author. The author guarantees all contents are original and do not infringe upon the legal rights of any other person or work. No part of this book may be reproduced in any form without the permission of the author.

Due to the changing nature of the Internet, if there are any web addresses, links, or URLs included in this manuscript, these may have been altered and may no longer be accessible. The views and opinions shared in this book belong solely to the author and do not necessarily reflect those of the publisher. The publisher therefore disclaims responsibility for the views or opinions expressed within the work.

Paperback ISBN-13: 978-1-66286-945-7
Ebook ISBN-13: 978-1-66286-946-4

It was a cool, windy day when John left the coast of Long Island, New York. Being late September, the water temperature was usually between fifty to sixty-eight degrees.

His trip would be approximately 2,500 miles to the Azores, specifically, the island of Pico, known for the highest mountain in Portugal (Ponta do Pico) and also known for its vineyards.

John and his wife, Gracie, visited Pico many times. They would anchor off the coast and visit the small towns and marvel at the black lava with green moss on it.

Gracie was a scuba diver and spent many hours in the crystal clear water. John was an avid fisherman, catching and cooking dinner many times.

The island of Pico was their vacation destination for many years until Gracie passed away from breast cancer only months ago.

Gracie was a registered nurse for twenty-five years. She worked at Winthrop-University Hospital. She had seen many births and deaths and everything in-between. Being a compassionate woman, it was the perfect occupation for her.

Also being a Christian woman, people would gravitate to her, and she comforted many patients with her faith in their time of need. Her parents were devout Christians and sent her to Stony-Brook Christian School, whose motto was "Character before career." The school, established in 1922, was still in operation.

When it came time to choose a career, she believed her only choice was nursing. Helping people was her "motto." She was a very firm believer in God and His Son, Jesus Christ.

Unfortunately, later in life, she developed breast cancer. She was diagnosed with stage VI.

Some months later, it turned into stage IV. As her health slowly deteriorated, she always kept her faith. Every day, she would wake up and say, "Another beautiful day."

Her faith gave her a certain calmness, which John could not understand. Gracie endlessly taxed to get him interested in the Christian religion, but he would have none of it. She would always say, "There's a Bible on my dresser whenever you're ready." But he had no interest in any religion.

As Gracie's time grew nearer and she got weaker, John was devastated. He couldn't do anything but sit and be by her side.

On her last day, she took his hand and said her last goodbye, and she said, "Faith is the best of things. Promise me you will try to accept and study the Word." But John was too upset to speak, then Gracie passed peacefully and quietly.

At the funeral were a couple of close friends, and they could see John was devastated. His best friend, Mitch, gave his condolences and said Gracie was like a sister to him. "I've known her since you two got together," he told John. "As long as I'm alive, I'll be here for you." Indeed, Mitch was his best friend.

Mitch practically dragged John out to a small pub in town. They both ordered Gracie's favorite wine (Elderberry). They both toasted Gracie and, with no inhibitions, cried.

At the end of the evening, John turned to Mitch and said, "Only with a true friend can I release my true feelings." Mitch agreed.

About a week later, John woke up one morning and the phone rang, and it was Mitch. He said, "I'm calling to see how you are doing?" John replied, "My heart is on the floor, and somehow, I'm finding the strength to keep breathing."

Mitch replied, "You have to start moving on with the rest of your life. It's not over yet." John said, "I don't know how without Gracie." Mitch said, "What was Gracie's last request?"

John said, "To study the Word." Mitch said, "That would be a great place to start. You have nothing to lose and everything to gain. You might find peace and a reason to go on."

John said, "I'll try, but it will not be easy. I've never thought about God or Jesus or any religion."

Mitch said, "Find a Bible and start with Genesis." John said, "I'll try for Gracie."

John found a Bible on Gracie's dresser and started reading Genesis. He got through how God created the earth in six days and rested on the seventh.

He stopped reading and thought, How can I believe these things I've never seen or heard! God, speak to me. I've always done everything on my own, worked hard for my money, and never asked for any help. I'm a self-made man.

He said out loud, "If you're listening, Gracie, I can't believe these things. I'm sorry." And he wondered, Is it inherent in all of us to know there is a God? Is it inherent in us all to know right from wrong and good from evil?

Have I been so blind all these years?

John called Mitch for a sit down meeting and explained to Mitch he could not accept or understand the Word. "I'll pray for you, brother, to see the light and truth." "Thank you," Mitch replied.

John said, "I'm going to take a trip to Pico, where Gracie and I spent a lot of time together. They were the best of times." Mitch said, "If you want company, I could probably get away for a while. You shouldn't go by yourself if it could be dangerous."

John said, "Thanks, but I can't expect you to drop everything. I know you have a lot going on." John said, "Don't worry, I'm a seasoned sailor, with years of experience. And if an emergency comes up, I have safety equipment, a dinghy, life preservers, and flares. At this point in my life, I'm just not worried about it. I'll be leaving in a couple of days. I hope you'll come see me off." "Of course," replied Mitch.

The day came for John to leave, and Mitch showed up early in the morning, the time when you could still see the moon and dawn was breaking.

"Ahoy!" yelled Mitch, and John's head popped out of the cabin. He said, "Just getting things ready to leave." Mitch, noticing the weather didn't look too good, said, "I don't like the look of the sky. It looks dark on the horizon." John answered and said, "Oh well, there's always a storm somewhere. I'll be ok." They said their goodbyes, and John pulled up anchor, and Mitch yelled, "I'll pray the Lord look after you!" as he watched John sail off into darkness.

Mitch, thinking to himself, thought, I'm worried about him. The weather doesn't look good, and he's not thinking right.

John's fifty-foot vessel had three sails that filled up with wind as soon as he hoisted them up. The vessel was his pride and joy. He took very good care of it and lovingly named it "Gracie."

About an hour out, the wind did not ease up like he thought it would. Looking out at the horizon, now the sky looked darker.

Heading on a southeast course, he thought he would skirt around the storm. But as the hours passed, the storm was growing, and his anemometer wind scale read twenty-five knots and climbing. The waves were approximately twenty feet now. Still battling the storm, his weather radio said the wind could be forty-eight knots and higher, with the possibility of reaching over 10 on the Beaufort scale.

A short while later, the sky grew darker. The waves were at least fifty-feet tall now, he estimated. The rain was driving now, and the waves were smashing against the bow. The vessel was like being on a rollercoaster, going up to the top and down the valleys. He decided to take down the aft and front sails, with the main sail up for direction purposes, which seemed to work for a short time. Then all of a sudden, the wind intensified again.

When he came to the top of another wave, he could see the light from another ship in the distance. Going down another valley now, he tried to keep a bearing on the other ship. When he crested the wave, he could see flares coming off the ship. Trying to navigate toward the other ship, he crested another wave, but the ship was gone.

Thinking, Now, this could be bad, he rushed to put on his life preserver. He held on to the vessel's wheel as tight as he could. With the wind at hurricane force now, he heard the mast making a cracking noise he'd never heard before.

All of a sudden, the mast broke in two and crashed on top of the cabin, totally destroying it. He thought, All of my supplies are gone.

He realized he was in a fight for his life and his vessel.

With his hand locked on to the vessel's wheel, he thought, There's nothing I can do, and there's no time anyway.

The next moment, a huge wave came and raised the bow and flipped the vessel over on its top. Another wave came and righted the vessel. He was in the scorching rain and wind again. Then he saw a massive wave coming and thought, Should I try to get in what's left of the cabin? But what if the vessel goes under? I'll be trapped.

So, he held onto the vessel's wheel the best he could. The giant hit, and he was thrust into the water. He went under the waves and fought to break the surface. This went on for a while. Finally, he watched his vessel go under the waves. The last part he could see was the bow and the name "Gracie."

He bobbed up and down for hours, which seemed like an eternity. Being exhausted now, he couldn't fall asleep from the fear of going under the water.

Finally, the sea calmed down. The storm was passing slowly. He thought, I survived! Not knowing where he was, now he didn't even know which way to even try to swim to shipping lanes.

Darkness set in now. He could see the stars and a couple of airliners going by. Thinking, I have no flares or beacon, they'll never see me anyway. I have no food or water, and nobody knows where I am. The storm must have thrown me off course.

Thinking, Is this my end? To starve to death or die of thirst?

Now he was all alone somewhere in the middle of the Atlantic ocean.

Treading water for hours now, he kept scanning the ocean for any sings of a ship, a light, anything! Now there was nothing.

At first light, he noticed something moving on the surface of the water; it was a shark fin. Being a fisherman for years, he knew the different types of shark; this was a bull shark. This shark could potentially be a man eater. He could tell it was a bull shark by the front and rear fins.

The shark came within inches of him at a high rate of speed. The shark turned around and came back at him, this time at a slower speed, and he could see the eyes of the predator looking at him. Moments later, another shark came by, then another. He thought by staying completely still, they would lose interest, but they didn't leave. They started bumping him and nudging him. So he started yelling as loud as he could and hitting the water with his hands.

This seemed to scare them away for a short time, but now he could see they were encircling him. He counted about eight sharks. With the feeling of dread and his impending death, the thought of being eaten alive, he decided to try and drown himself, but the will to live was too strong. He thought about how hard he worked all of his life and all of his possessions and his stocks and different bank accounts, and he wondered what it was all about. All the money couldn't help him now. Then his thoughts turned to Gracie and their life together, and he remembered her last words to him: "To study the Word and faith is the best of things." He promised her he would try and open his mind and heart, which was very hard for him. Material possessions were the focus of his life.

He said out loud, "I'll try, Gracie," and he looked up to the sky and yelled, "God, if You're here and listening, please help me! I don't want to die like this. I'm afraid to die, forgive me for never believing!" The next moment, he noticed the sharks were gone!

Suddenly, he felt something under his feet. It felt firm but smooth. Slowly, he was raised above the water line, and he could see it was a huge humpback whale. Seconds later, another whale to his right and another on his left. They were making whooping and whistling sounds; he realized they were singing.

They were very calm in the water, and all at once, they all started moving in the same direction slowly. A feeling of calm came over him that he'd never felt before, and he realized his prayers were answered.

Then he heard a voice. He couldn't tell if it was in his head or out from the sea. And the voice said, "John, why are you here? This isn't where I want you!" He didn't know how to answer and laid down on the whale's back and passed out from the ordeal he was spared from.

After hours of sleep, he woke up and realized, "I'm still alive!" The three huge humpbacks kept him alive and safe from the predators of the deep. He knew they were sent from God. He instinctively knew this was true. Also, Genesis was true, and now he knew who spoke to him the previous night; it was Jesus Christ, the Son of God. Then he prayed to the Lord for forgiveness and said to Jesus, "I believe You are the Son of God and died on the cross for my sins! I praise You and thank You!"

Still being exhausted and having a new sense of calm, he fell asleep again. Later, he was awoken by water being splashed on him from the whale's blowhole, and he could hear a ship's airhorn off in the distance.

The whales were moving at a faster pace now and met the ship. It was a Coast Guard cutter out on patrol. The whales got him within fifty feet of the ship. The captain sent a life boat to retrieve John. The crew members were out on deck, taking pictures and videos. The moment John was rescued, the whales disappeared under the waves.

At this time, John was dehydrated and very hungry. He said, "This is not the time for questions please," and they brought him to the ship's infirmary. He had a small meal and fell asleep again.

When he finally woke up and gathered his senses, the captain said, "We have questions." John laughed and said, "I'm sure."

The captain said, "In all my years in service, I never have seen anything like this. Three humpback whales, and a man sitting in the middle of them." Then John recounted his ordeal, and the captain replied, "Amazing!"

The chaplain said, "I believe you were saved, and maybe it's time for a change in your life."

John replied, "I've already changed. It took a lot for me to see the truth, but this is real."

When John got back home, he pondered his ordeal for a time and realized this was the most important event in his life so far.

With spring a couple weeks away, now he went out and bought a brand new fifty-foot, three sail vessel, which he lovingly named "Gracie II."

He knew he had to take this trip to Pico again for a lot of reasons. The sea was calling to him. He always said the magic of the sea was something to behold.

He set a date to leave and wanted a meeting with his best friend, Mitch. So they met at the same small pub in town, but this time, it was under different circumstances.

At this meeting, there were some surprises for Mitch that he didn't expect. John divulged all the details, and Mitch was amazed.

John told Mitch, "When all was lost, I called to God, and He answered me and sent the three humpback whales to save me. That's not all. The night the whales arrived, somebody spoke to me." Mitch said, "Who? Who was it?" John replied, "Jesus Christ!" Mitch said, "Did you see him?" John said, "No, I didn't have to. I knew in my heart and soul who it was." Then he told Mitch what the Lord said. "The basic idea is, I'm not doing His work. The Lord changed my mind and heart. I'm a new man and a free man now, and I have peace."

Then John explained he changed his last will and testament to include charity and said, "Money isn't the most important thing in life. This life is short and fleeting, and I think one of the most important things is helping people if you can."

John told Mitch he was leaving in the morning and asked him to come see him off. Mitch replied, "I wouldn't miss it."

The next morning, Mitch showed up early and wished him a safe journey. John said, "No worries, whatever happens, I'm a new man with a new mind and heart. I'm born again."

Mitch replied, "I envy you," and smiled, and they both waved goodbye.

Now leaving port off Bayshore, Long Island, New York, the sun was glistening off the water, the sun was out, and a slight breeze. It was a beautiful day. About ten minutes out, a white dove landed on the bowsprit of the vessel. He wondered, "Are not indigenous to this part of the country." About an hour out, the bird was still there. He thought, Maybe I should try to catch the dove to keep it safe.

LASt

Moments later, he turned and took a last look at the island. When he turned to check on the dove, it was gone. He looked up in the air and in the water and on deck. The dove had disappeared, vanished into thin air!

He contemplated this and all of the recent events in his life, what changed him into a new man. He realized the dove was a gift! With tears in his eyes and a smile on his face at the same time, he shouted out loud.

"I love you, Gracie! I made it!"

The End.

www.ingramcontent.com/pod-product-compliance
Lightning Source LLC
LaVergne TN
LVHW021743060526
838200LV00052B/3443